WHEN TIME RUNS OUT:

TARA'S QUEST FOR VENGEANCE

DIANA CARTER

When Time Runs Out: Tara's Quest for Vengeance

Mystery/Family Drama

All Rights Reserved

Copyright © 2018 by Diana Carter

LET'S DO THIS PUBLISHING, LLC
P.O. Box 300795
Drayton Plaines, MI 48330

ISBN 13: 978-0-9997106-6-1

Cover Designed by Professional Instant Printing. All Rights Reserved

PRINTED IN THE UNITED STATES OF AMERICA

OTHER BOOKS WRITTEN BY DIANA CARTER
BROKEN PROMISES SERIES

Book 1

Book 2
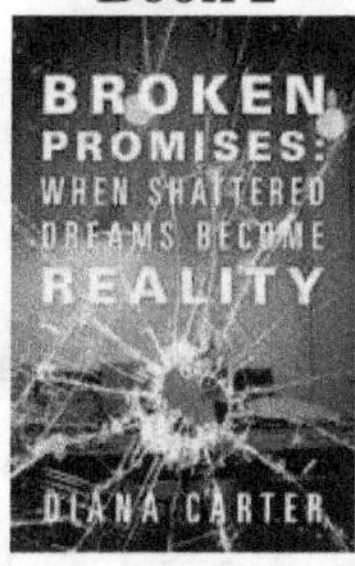

Book 3

Spin-Off

Dark Revenge:
The Trey Taylor Story

Never a Dull Moment:
The Nick Jr. Story
The Sister Factor Spin-Off

THE SISTER FACTOR SERIES

Book 1

Book 2

Book 3

Book 4

<u>Dedication</u>

This book is dedicated in loving memory of the many people that have been influential in my life:

My loving parents: John & Eunice Williams

My loving sisters: Julia Kate Jackson
                       Marcella Leona Williams
                       Tina Marie Williams

My loving brothers: John Lee Williams
                       Franklin Delano Roosevelt Williams
                       Otis Williams
                       Larry Williams
                       Randy Lee Williams

My friend/mentor   Michael Allen McKinney

Acknowledgements

I will like to acknowledge, God as the guiding force in my life. I will always praise Him as my Lord and Savior. I am truly blessed for His seeing fit to bless me with the gift of words. May He continue to bless me with the ability to write novels that are enjoyable and entertaining. My truest hope is to be blessed with many more years of writing for my family, friends, and readers.

I am very thankful for the creation of Let's Do This Publishing, LLC (LDTPLLC).

L is for **love** that makes the world go around

D is for **Destiny** the brightest star that has brought light to my life

T is for **Tutti** (aka Annette Hollings) who was so important in helping me deal with issues in my younger years

P is for **Perfection** – The one and only Jesus Christ

L is for **life** and adjusting to the many challenges

L is for **loyalty** what bonds people together

C is for **Cornell** the best baby brother a person could have

Lastly, I would like to acknowledge and thank the many readers of ***Dark Revenge: The Trey Taylor Story*** for giving me feedback on who should be featured if a sequel was written for this title. ***When Time Runs Out: Tara's Quest for Vengeance*** was a joy to write because of this character's passionate beliefs. It would be great if everyone had a Tara in their life that believed in them no matter what the circumstances. Please note how much I appreciate the feedback of my readers. This allows me to create dynamic storylines that is great entertainment for all. Thank you all for giving me the inspiration to continue to write.

God's blessing,

Diana Carter

When Time Runs Out: Tara's Quest for Vengeance

Chapter One

Tara rolled over in bed to look at her cell phone to see who had the nerve to call her this late at night. When she saw Keshawn's (her boyfriend's) number she was ready to give him a piece of her mind. He knew she had trouble sleeping since her best friend Tia went missing. He went to the doctor's office with her to get sleeping pills. Rolling over saying a sleepy hello, Tara listen to what Keshawn was saying.

"Can you repeat that, baby?" Tara asked sitting up in bed.

"I said I need you to get up and get dressed. I'm coming by, we found Tia." Keshawn repeated.

"Thank you, Jesus. I will be ready in ten minutes." Tara ended the call before Keshawn had a chance to say anything else.

Thinking, as she freshen up and got dressed, Tara couldn't wait to give Tia a piece of her mind, *"On my God, thank you, Jesus for answering my prayers. This is the best news I've had in weeks."*

Tara thought about the ten days that went by since anyone heard or saw Tia. She had come close to ripping Tony's (Tia's no good ex-boyfriend's) head off. She thought that low-life had something to do with Tia's disappearance. Trey and Jerome (her older brother and his best friend) had to follow her around for a few days to ensure she didn't run up on Tony. Tony was a street hood that had no respect for women. Some of his illegal activities should have landed him in jail.

Tara was getting restless waiting on Keshawn. She wished he hurry up and get there. While she was waiting she decided to take a minute to think about how she was going to approach Tia. What she really wanted to do was tear her apart for worrying her like that, but she knew she was going to be too happy to see her. Coming out of her thoughts when she heard the intercom buzz, Tara grabbed her coat and purse after she pressed the buzzer. She just wanted to go see her best friend.

Tara was surprised to see Trey and Jerome standing behind Keshawn. Taking a minute to see the look on their faces gave Tara the shivers. Trey moved around the other two men and went to stand in front of Tara holding both of her hands. Tara didn't wait for Trey to say one word before she started crying and shaking her head. All she kept saying was no. Trey hugged Tara for a few minutes then helped her to the sofa.

"Tara, I'm so sorry, but Tia's body was found in a wooded area at Jefferson Park." Trey whispered.

"Trey, you have to be mistaken. I want to see this person, because it can't be Tia." Tara said.

"Baby girl, I'm sorry. Her mom already confirmed it was Tia."

"I'm not taking the word of that horrid woman. She hasn't paid attention to Tia in years."

"I know you're in shock, but it's Tia." Trey said.

"Baby, do you need me to stay here with you the rest of the night?" Keshawn asked.

"You can stay here if you want to, but I'm going to see the person you guys insist is my best friend." Tara stood and headed for the door. Trey and Jerome caught up to her before she could leave out.

"Tara, we need you to take it easy. You don't want to do this tonight." Jerome said.

"Get your hands off of me, Jerome, you too, Trey. I should have killed that bastard as soon as we found out Tia was missing."

"We don't know what happened to Tia, baby girl."

"Don't baby girl, me. I should have taken care of this the minute I found out she was missing. I may have been able to save her." Tara said with tears rolling down her face.

"Honey, you couldn't control what happened to Tia. She had a lot of things going on in her life that only she could deal with." Keshawn said.

"I don't want to hear that shit right now. I need all of you to leave."

"Tara, we are not going anywhere. I know you're upset, but we will help you find out what happened to Tia." Trey said.

"I don't need any help. I will do this on my own. I told all of you many times that we should be doing more to find Tia, but you guys just swept it under the rug like she didn't matter."

"You need to be reasonable, Tara. Tia disappeared many times without contacting you. Don't put this on us like we didn't care about her." Trey was getting a little inpatient with his baby sister.

Tara calmed down and thought about what Trey said and asked, "So what happens next?"

"The crime scene is secured. We will know more after her official cause of death is determined." Keshawn answered.

"I want to go to the crime scene." Tara said.

"I can get you clearance first thing in the morning." Keshawn said.

"That's not good enough. I want to go now." Tara insisted.

"Baby girl, please get some rest tonight. JW and I will be here first thing in the morning to take you to the crime scene." Trey said. He always called Jerome JW.

Thinking again, Tara said, "Ok, you guys head on home. I know Linda is wondering what's keeping you out so late, Trey." Malinda was Trey's wife (everyone calls her Linda).

None of the men were buying that Tara was going to sit tight, so Keshawn said, "I'll stay here with, Tara. See you guys in the morning."

"You can leave too, Keshawn. I need to rest."

"I don't think so, Tara." Keshawn said.

"I don't need a babysitter. Go home, Keshawn."

"Tara, you shouldn't be alone. You can let Keshawn stay or you can come home with me." Trey insisted.

"Fine, you can stay, Keshawn, but I want to be alone." Tara went into her bedroom and slammed the door.

<u>Chapter Two</u>

Tara had a restless night. She had every intention of waiting Keshawn out, but he made her take a sleeping pill. The main reason she gave in was because she knew that he was right. It would have been pointless to go to the scene last night because they would not be able to collect any evidence until daylight.

Tara was lucky because she had the chance to choose the crime scenes to work because of a special provision in her Internship Agreement with the Chicago Police Department. She was working on her Master's degree at Northwestern University. She was approached by other top universities, but she didn't want to leave home or Trey's private investigation firm. She was noticed by the police department when she worked on Trey's case a few years ago when he was falsely accused of murdering his ex-girlfriend.

Tara heard Keshawn in the kitchen. The smells in the apartment told her, he was cooking breakfast. It was a waste of time, because she wasn't going to waste time eating when she needed to find out what happened to her best friend. She was trying to be patient, but Trey and Jerome was taking their sweet time getting there to pick her up. She decided to give them fifteen minutes. If they weren't there, she and

Keshawn were going to leave without them. Ten minutes later she heard the doorbell and rushed out of her bedroom. Seeing Tameka (Tia's mom) instead of the guys irritated Tara.

"Why are you here instead of finding out who murdered my baby?" Tameka asked Keshawn.

"Lady, you have a lot of nerve barging in here demanding anything. Don't pretend you cared about Tia." Tara said angrily.

"She was my, baby. What the hell you mean I didn't care about her?" Tameka responded.

"I came to you more than once asking for your help to get her away from that abusive fool, but you didn't lift one finger to help."

"Don't put this on me, little girl. I told her to stay away from Tony, but as usual she didn't listen."

"Why would she when you were criticizing her all the time? In all the years I've known Tia not once did I see you help her when it didn't benefit you." Tara responded.

"Ladies, this isn't getting us anywhere. I think you should leave, Ms. Thomas." Keshawn said.

"Gladly, I guess I have to get my information from the police." Tameka said. As Tameka was leaving, Trey and Jerome arrived, "I hope you can talk sense into your sister, Trey." Tameka said as she rushed out the door.

"Wow, what was she doing here?" Trey asked.

"Being fake as hell as usual, pretending to care about Tia."

"Tara, we need to talk before we head out to the crime scene." Trey said.

"Trey, I don't want you guys babying me. I want to know everything that is going on."

"I think you need to take a step back from this case. Dad called me this morning. He doesn't want you to get involved."

"I knew this was going to happen. Did you have my back, Trey?" Tara asked.

"Tara, I will always have your back. I couldn't sleep last night, so I did a little investigating of my own. Tara, Tia was involved in some shady dealings."

"I don't want to hear this, Trey. I'm not going to stop until I find out what happened to Tia. We need to put more pressure on Tony."

"Tara, you know Tony was the prime suspect when Tia first disappeared, but now I'm thinking there is more going on here." Trey said.

"Tara, TT is right. These are some dangerous people we're talking about." Jerome said, calling Trey by his nickname he gave him years ago.

"Trey, I need to know how Tia died." Tara said.

"The autopsy results are not in, but we know she was shot several times, had severe head injuries, and may have been sexually assaulted." Trey explained.

Tears falling down her face, Tara said angrily, "She was treated like trash. I'm not letting this go, Trey. How long have she been dead?"

"Nothing is official yet, but they are guessing about forty-eight hours."

"I can't take this any longer. Take me to the crime scene please." Tara said.

"I agree with, Trey, Tara. I think you should leave this one alone." Keshawn added.

"Let's go." Tara grabbed her coat and purse and walked out of the apartment.

Chapter Three

Captain Carl Marshall sat at his desk looking over the preliminary results of Tia Thomas's murder case. He usually didn't get involved with cases like this one. He found letting his detectives do their thing worked out much better then him sticking his nose where it didn't belong. But sitting at his desk thinking about that poor young woman suffering unthinkable trauma sadden him.

He didn't know how his prized intern, Tara Taylor was going to handle what happened to her best friend. He hated to admit it, but he still missed her brother Trey being on the force. He would have had such a promising career if he had been patient and let things go he couldn't change. Carl could see that Tara inherited her brother's quick instincts that will take her far in her career as a CSI (Crime Scene Investigator).

When Tara first approached him about being an Intern, he almost turned her down because of the events that happened when Trey was on trial for murder. Just like then, Tara wouldn't stop as soon as they realized Tia was missing. After convincing Tia's mom to file a missing person report three days after her disappearance, Tara started her own investigation in which Carl had to reel her in more than once.

Sometimes it felt like the old days when he had to stay on Trey for bending rules to his advantage.

Tara was the best CSI person, he ran across in a long time. She was still young and had a few things to learn, especially about being tactful. She could evaluate a crime scene in no time and had the eyes and nose to sniff out clues that wasn't apparent. Carl personally made sure the crime scene was preserved as best as possible. He knew his best detective and Tara's boyfriend (Keshawn) had his work cut out for him, keeping Tara from working the scene last night.

Carl was strongly thinking about taking Tara off this case. She was good, but emotional when someone close to her was involved. It was Carl's guess that Tara didn't know some of the seedy things the deceased appeared to be involve in. Tara not getting along with Tia's mom was also going to create a big problem. Legally Tameka Thomas was the next of kin even though she and her daughter were estranged.

Carl was also dreading working closely with Trey again. He still regretted not being able to convince Trey to stay on the force. Thinking about Trey and his murder case brought to the forefront that Carl wasn't always the best judge of characters. He had no idea his best friend, Christopher Young, father of the murdered victim was so far gone that he was one of the individuals responsible for framing Trey for his daughter's murder. Carl thoughts were interrupted when Tara and her gang knocked on his door.

"Captain, I want to know why I was denied access to the crime scene." Tara said.

"Good morning to you too, Intern Taylor."

"How is it a good morning when I'm not allowed to do my job?" Tara asked.

"I figured it was time for us to talk about your role in the case. Detective Konner, please escort Trey and Jerome to the waiting room." Carl ordered.

"No, they need to stay since they will take an active part in the case, Captain." Tara said.

"That's not your call, Intern Taylor. As more details are uncovered I feel that this case is loaded with unknowns. It may be too dangerous for you since you were close to the deceased."

"With all due respect, Captain, I disagree." Tara said.

"Carl, cut to the chase. Your problem is not my sister's involvement in this case, but that our firm will be assisting." Trey added.

"Listen, I don't need the two of you telling me what my motives are for this case. Intern Taylor, you have already proven that you have problems with the deceased mom and ex-boyfriend. Sometimes I think you let your personal feelings clog your judgment."

"Tony is a disgusting thug and Tameka didn't give a damn about Tia. I had to force her to make a missing persons report." Tara defended herself.

"That is exactly what I'm talking about. Your animosity for these people can put you in a dangerous position." Carl clarified.

"Ok, may I be allowed to work the crime scene and not have any interactions with any suspects in the case?" Tara asked.

"That sounds reasonable. Trey what would be your and Jerome's involvement? Carl asked.

"We won't have any specific involvement besides being a backup for Tara. We want to make sure she is safe." Trey explained.

"Ok, I will give you guys' access to the scene. Detective Konner, escort them to the scene and take Barnes and Webster with you."

"Sure thing, Captain, we will report our findings as soon as possible." Keshawn said.

"Don't make me regret this, Intern Taylor."

"Thank you, Captain."

"Konner make sure there are not any problems." Carl said. As they left his office Carl had the feeling that Tara didn't mean one word she promised him.

<u>Chapter Four</u>

When they arrived at the crime scene tears formed in Tara eyes. On the way over, Tara received a call from Tameka. She couldn't believe that foolish woman wanted to have Tia cremated. There was no way Tara was going to let that happened. Tara promised to pay for the funeral since Tia didn't have any insurance. Tameka also extorted an extra thousand dollars for her own personal expenses. Tameka was going to meet them back at Trey's office later in the afternoon. She told Tara she would have to make all the arrangements and that the casket had to be closed because of Tia's condition.

The crime scene tape that Tara had become accustom to seeing was eerie. She understood where the Captain was coming from. Knowing that she was working the scene where her best friend was found was much different than when she was investigating a stranger case. Looking around the area Tara dried her tears and went to work. Just looking around the scene, Tara knew Tia wasn't murdered there. Someone had dumped her there.

Trey and Jerome gave Tara her space to work. They decided to go to a nearby park bench. The weather was cold seeing that it was only thirty-one degrees. Keshawn and the two officers worked outside of the taped off area to give Tara room to collect evidence. From the report Tara was given, she knew that only the two officers that was working with Keshawn had access to the crime scene. There was hardly any blood at the crime scene.

Tara worked for a few hours collecting evidence. Once she was done the two officers and Keshawn went back to the station while she, Trey, and Jerome headed to the morgue. Tameka had given the morgue director permission for the trio to view Tia's body. Trey didn't want Tara to view the body, but she wouldn't be deterred.

On the drive to the morgue Tara talked to Trey and Jerome about having the service the upcoming Saturday. She wanted their Pastor to preside. Tara was still upset that they couldn't find anything to connect Tony to Tia's disappearance or murder. Pulling up in front of the morgue the trio went inside. After meeting a few minutes with the director, they were taken to this cold isolated room. When Tia's body was pulled out, Tara took a deep breath. She knew her friend was badly beaten, so she tried to prepare herself for the worse. The sheet was pulled down to right above Tia's breast. At first sight of her friend, Tara almost passed out. She had seen dead bodies before, but seeing her best friend lying on that cold slab was heartbreaking.

Tia's beautiful face was almost unrecognizable. The bullet holes in her upper chest were unnerving. Tara knew Tameka was right. They were going to have a closed casket. Staying there a few minutes longer, Tara told Trey and Jerome she was ready to leave. They were headed back to the office, but Trey and Jerome had outside business so they dropped Tara off. Tara sat at her computer to download the evidence she collected and make arrangements for Tia's funeral. Beverly, Trey's assistant offered her condolences and asked what she could do to help.

"Thanks for the offer, Bev, but I don't need any help right now. I'll let you know when I get everything situated." Tara promised. Tara work at her computer for the remainder of the day before heading home.

Trey and Tara was summoned over to the big house later that evening. Tara started not to go because she knew what her parents were up to. No one was going to talk her into giving this case up. Somebody had to get justice for Tia. It most certainly wasn't going to be Tameka. All she cared about was getting a big payday. Tameka was dumb enough to ask the police if Tia had life insurance. Pulling up at her parents' house, Tara noticed that Trey was already there. Tara was put out when she also noticed Talia (her older sister) car in the driveway. The two of them didn't get along, so she wondered what the heck she was doing there. Entering the house she heard her family voices coming from the family room.

Tanya, Tara's mom stood and greeted her daughter, "I know your ears were burning, we were just talking about you."

"Hi, Mom, how are all you guys doing and why were you all talking about me?" Tara asked.

"Don't play dumb with us, girl." Trenton, their dad said.

"What are you talking about, Dad?" Tara questioned.

"You being hard headed and not listening to your brother by staying away from this case." Trenton said.

Tara glanced at Trey, and Trey held his hands up, "Dad, I have to see this thought. That mother of hers isn't trying to get justice for Tia. She is just looking for a big payday."

"Speaking of payday, I heard that you are paying for the funeral and other incidentals for that woman." Tanya said.

Glancing at Trey again, Trenton said, "Don't look at your brother. He has been tight lipped. He hasn't told us anything. We had a visit from that skank."

"Trent name calling isn't necessary." Tanya told her husband.

"All I know is, you should sit your behind down somewhere, Tara and let the police do their job." Talia added.

"I don't need or want any advice from you. If this happened to Linda, you wouldn't sit back and wait for bits and pieces of information." Tara said.

"Tara, this has nothing to do with my wife. As I told you when all of this happened, there are a lot of unknowns and we need to take a step back." Trey said. Talia was Trey's wife Malinda (Linda) best friend.

"Trey, I understand if you want to take a step back, but I have no intentions of doing so." Tara insisted.

"Well in that case, I'm sorry, Dad. We are not going to let Tara take this on by herself." Trey said.

"Little girl it's time you grow up and stop thinking about what you want all the time. Trey you need to stop defending her. She almost cost you your marriage during your trial." Talia said.

"That's not true and you know it, Talia. If Linda had more faith in her husband, he wouldn't have had such a hard time back then." Tara said.

"That's enough girls. I hope you know what you are doing, Tara. I think we should all sleep on this and revisit at another time when TJ and Trevor can be here." Tanya said.

"I love all you guys, but I need to be able to sleep at night. I won't be able to do that until I find out what happened to Tia. Trev taught me how to defend myself along with the training I had with the police department." Tara said. The meeting was called to a close, and they said their goodbyes.

<u>Chapter Five</u>

Tara woke up the morning after the meeting with her family. She didn't sleep well last night. She appreciated Trey and Jerome checking up on her, but she just needed time to think. Tears formed in her eyes as she thought about the last time she saw Tia. They talked about what they were going to do for their birthdays. Tia was ten days older than Tara, so she always tried to boss Tara around. Next month they would have been celebrating their twenty-third birthdays.

"I think we should celebrate at the Sound Board. My brother TJ would be able to get us the hook-up." Tara said.

"Why do you want to go to that up-tight boogie place? Let's go someplace we can meet some gangster style guys." Tia responded.

"You know that is not going to work. I have my man, why would I go looking for anything else? And you know you are not going to step out on Tony."

"Tony and I are done. I finally realized that you were right. I do deserve a man who will love me unconditionally and I think I may have found him."

"I hope you mean that this time, Tia. I'm scared for you every time you go back to Tony. Wait a minute are you seeing someone?"

Tia intentionally ignore Tara's question, "I was afraid to leave him, but I had to pick my poison because I was more afraid of staying with him. He had started to be downright disrespectful."

"What did you expect from someone from the streets, Tia? Roger really loved you. I wished you had stayed with him. Are you back with Roger?"

Ignoring Tara's question again Tia said, "Me too, Tara, I gave up on him because I needed more excitement. Tony gave me excitement alright. Along with broken ribs, black eyes, STDs..."

"Okay, let's get together tomorrow." Tara suggested.

Tomorrow never came because two days later Tara realized Tia was missing. Why did this have to happen to Tia now that she finally decided to get rid of that loser? Tara was not giving up on Tony because she had a gut feeling he was responsible for what happened to Tia. Even if he didn't murder her, he was involved in some way. Guys like Tony aren't going to let a woman they considered their property to just walk away. Tony had controlled Tia for three years. He probably flipped out when he finally realized she was done with him. Tara knew Tia meant every word she said. That was the main reason Tara wasn't going to let up on Tony.

Trey and Jerome met in the conference room to discuss the case and the best way to contain Tara. Trey knew that would be next to impossible, but he wasn't about to let his baby sister get hurt. Trey asked Jerome to meet him before Tara arrived. They needed a plan to stay close to Tara at all times. She didn't know or Trey hoped she didn't know he had someone keeping an eye on her. Tara's attitude at the meeting was what he remembered when she fought so hard to prove his innocence years ago when he was framed for Sonya's murder.

"Man, Tara is on that one-track thing again. You should have seen her buff up against all of us yesterday, especially Talia." Trey said.

"You know this isn't going to be easy. Tia had a lot going on in her life and once Tara finds out the entire story she is going to be devastated." Jerome responded.

"Tell me about it. I had to redirect her from getting all over Linda's case again."

Jerome said with a smirk on his face, "That girl is never going to like your wife is she?"

"Doesn't look like it. It seems like she is never going to get along with Talia neither. I thought she was going to get up and smack Talia for a minute."

"I bet you thought when she got involved with Keshawn she would mellow out some. It seems to me that she is more possessive of you."

"I guess old habits die hard. So let's go over the shit Tia got herself mixed up in so we can figure out a way to keep Tara safe." Trey said. The guys worked for about an hour when Bev knocked and said Trey's older brother Trevor was there to see him. She showed him into the conference room. Trey was worried when he saw how upset Trevor seemed.

"Hey, Trev is everything okay?" Trey asked.

"I need to talk to you guys. Is Tara here? Trevor asked looking around.

"No not right now. We expect her later this afternoon." Jerome answered.

"Can we keep this visit between the three of us?" Trevor asked.

"What's going on, Trev? You're not making sense." Trey asked.

"We'll, I know I should have come forward sooner, but I didn't want to get into trouble." Trevor said.

"Get in trouble about what, Trev? Why are you talking in circles, man?" Trey asked.

"Guys, I was hiding out Tia from the night she went missing until two days before her body was found." Trevor said.

Trey and Jerome looked at Trevor in shock. "Hold up a minute, you mean to tell me you knew where Tia was all the while our baby sister was going out of her mind with worry?" Trey asked.

"Yes, Tia begged me not to tell anyone. She was so scared and knew the people she was afraid of was probably keeping taps on Tara."

"I can't believe this is happening. When Tara finds out she's going to be all over you, man." Trey said.

"I know, I was hoping she wouldn't have to find out."

"That was an unwise choice you made, Trev." Jerome added.

"I know that now, but when Tia came to me that night she was dirty and hungry. I wanted her to go straight to Tara's, but she said that

Tara wouldn't understand and she didn't want Tara to get hurt because she was messing around with the wrong people."

"Trev, you're going to have to go to the police with this information. When was the last time you saw Tia?" Trey asked.

"It was two nights before her body was found around six o'clock. She was anxious and said that all of this would be cleared up soon after she had a meeting that night." Trevor explained.

"So let's see. That had to be Thursday the eighteenth. I think we need to take this meeting to your house or the gym. I want to have a plan when we break the news to Tara." Trey said.

"I know we have to tell her but it is going to be hard. I know she is going to be mad at me."

"Yes she is, but we have to deal with that later." Trey said as the trio headed out before Tara showed up at the office.

Chapter Six

Trey, Trevor, and Jerome arrived at Trevor's house thirty minutes later. Trevor offered the guys something to eat or drink, but they declined. Trey noticed that Trevor was still nervous. He worried that Trevor was in deeper than he led on at his office. Trey knew they were going to have a hard time getting Tara to understand why Trevor didn't let her know Tia's whereabouts. Now they were all sitting at Trevor's dining room table waiting on Trevor to open up.

"I know you guys are waiting on me to tell you what's going on. Before I get into all of that I need to tell you guys that Tia and I have been involved for the last few months."

"Involved how, Trev?" Trey asked.

"We were dating. We were planning on telling Tara soon, but both of us knew she would have a problem with our involvement. Before you guys say anything, I know I was too old for Tia."

"It's not about the age difference, Trev, but that you guys kept your relationship a secret." Jerome added.

"It just kind of happened. Tia started coming to the gym for self-defense classes. She was finally ready to leave Tony. She wanted to be able to protect herself and to stop depending on Tara so much."

"That all seems normal. Why not let Tara know what you guys were doing?" Trey was trying to understand.

"Tia felt Tara was losing faith in her because she didn't have the courage to leave Tony alone. Once she made up her mind to leave Tony for good, she started to receive threats." Trevor explained.

"Who was making the threats, Tony?" Jerome asked.

"At first that is what I thought, but then she went into hiding saying other people may be after her."

"Did she mention anyone by name?" Trey asked.

"No, but the last night I saw her she said she had to meet with someone that would make all of this go away and she would be free to come out of hiding."

"Trev, we have to take this to the police. Unfortunately, they may see you as a suspect. We need to get you a lawyer." Trey said.

Trevor was still nervous, "Why would they blame me for anything? I loved Tia. I wouldn't do anything to hurt her."

"I'm not sure what our next move should be. I know we have to bring Tara and the family in. TJ may be able to help us out legally too." Trey explained.

"So what you are saying, Trey is that I'm in big trouble?" Trevor said.

"Yes, with the law and our family. Tara is not in a good place right now. I know she would want to be on your side and to help you, but it will take her a minute to get over the fact that you kept Tia's whereabouts a secret. Trey said.

"Why don't we get with the family first? That way we can have support when Tara flips out. But we need to take care of this today and get Trev to the police station to make his statement." Jerome added.

"Trev, we will get you through this. I will call the family and see who will be able to meet us in a few hours. You need to rest. JW and I will stay here and we all can go over the Mom and Dad's once the family is together." Trey said.

"Thanks, guys. I've really been freaking out." Trevor left Trey and Jerome and went into his bedroom to rest for a while.

"This is going to be devastating for Tara. I don't know what she is going to say or do to Trev. Let's start making the calls." Trey said. He and Jerome contacted everyone and they planned on meeting with the family in three hours.

By the time Trey, Trevor, and Jerome walked into the big house the family was there waiting on them in the family room. They must have been talking about something heavy because Tara had this look on her face like this was the last place she wanted to be. Talia sat on the other side of the room. Their parents were sitting on the sofa with TJ sitting next to them. Trey thanked everyone for meeting them on short notice.

"What is this meeting about, Trey? Trenton asked.

"New evidence about Tia's case has been brought to our attention, but a family meeting was necessary before we go to the authorities." Trey responded.

"What new evidence, Trey?" Tara asked.

Glancing at Trevor for a second, Trey answered, "Well, it seems that Trev was in contact with Tia before her body was found." "

"Trev, when were you in contact with Tia?" Tara asked.

Trevor went to stand near Tara. "Tara, I need you to understand I was trying to do the right thing."

"I don't like the sound of this, Trev."

"Well, Tia and I were involved."

"Involved how, Trev?" Tara asked.

"We were in a relationship. She came to see me the night she disappeared. She was dirty and hungry. She said she needed me to hide her for a few days." Trevor explained.

Tara stood facing her brother, "Wait a minute. You mean to tell me you knew where Tia was all the time I was worried sick about her?"

"Yes, up until two days before her body was found, she was hiding out at my gym."

Tara walked closer to Trevor and Trey had to stand in between them. "Tara you need to hear, Trev out." Trey said.

"Calm down, Tara." Tanya took Tara's hand and led her over to the sofa.

"Trev, why didn't you tell the authorities?" TJ asked.

"I lost it when I found out Tia was dead. Then I was afraid to come forward because I thought they would view me as a suspect."

"You need a lawyer, Trevor." Trenton said. "Trey, can you check to see if Victoria is available?" Trenton said. Victoria was the lawyer that defended Trey at his murder trial.

"Sure, Dad, I was going to call her after this meeting"

"How could you do this, Trev? Tia was my best friend and you knew how worried I was about her." Tara asked with tears rolling down her face.

"I'm sorry, baby girl. I wanted to tell you about our relationship, but Tia said you wouldn't understand. She said you saw her as damaged goods and wouldn't welcome her into our family."

"I didn't see her as damaged goods, but a relationship between the two of you wasn't right. You're too old for her." Tara said. Trevor was thirteen years older than Tia.

"Lay off of him, Tara. This family needs to stop living their lives around how you would feel or react to things. That relationship was between Trev and Tia and none of your concern." Talia said.

"I don't want to hear your nonsense today, Talia. I had a right to know about that relationship."

"No, you didn't. The sooner you get that through your thick head, the sooner we will be able to help our brother."

"Cut it out right now girls. Both of you better learn how to get along with each other. TJ, Trevor, Trey, and Jerome, I need to see you guys in my office." Trenton said.

After the men left the room Tanya looked at her daughters with sadness. "Your dad is right. We can't continue to have these outbursts between the two of you every time we come together as a family." Tanya said.

"Well, tell Talia to stay in her lane. She is always butting in where she doesn't belong." Tara said.

"I have a right to speak my mind. The people in this family, especially the men need to stop babying you all the time."

"I'm not a baby. I can take care of myself. I have a right to speak my mind too. Trev was too old to me messing around with Tia."

"This is the last time I'm going to bring this up to the two of you. I'm going to take care of a few things and I expect the two of you to work this out. I will not tolerate this behavior any longer." Tanya said before she left the room. Trey came in a few minutes later.

"Tara we're headed to the police station. Tori will be on standby if we need her. We need to present a united from for Trev's sake. Our brother needs us." Trey gave Tara and Talia a brief hug before he left to escort Trevor to the police station.

Chapter Seven

Tara went to the police station with Trey, Trevor, and Jerome. Trenton and TJ stayed behind to see what they could do in case the police tried to charge Trevor with anything. Tara was still mad at Trevor for hiding Tia, but she took into consideration what the rest of her family was saying. She still felt that Trevor shouldn't have been involved with Tia, but she was glad to know Tia was finally done with Tony.

As soon as they walked into the station Keshawn met them in the front lobby. He wondered why all of them were there together, but Tara whispered to him that she would explain later and that they needed to see the Carl. Although Trey was her favorite brother, she had a close relationship with Trevor too. That is why she was so hurt he didn't tell her about his relationship with Tia. Once they were seated in the Captain's office he asked why they were there.

"Captain, my brother, Trevor have information regarding Tia's case." Tara said.

"Okay, I'm listening."

"During the time Tia was missing most of it she spent hiding out in my gym." Trevor said.

"Wait a minute. You knew where Ms. Thomas was at while she was a missing person?" Carl asked.

"Yes, she came to me that first night she went missing and said that she needed a place to hide out for a while. When I tried to get her to contact Tara, she panicked. She said that she didn't want to involve my sister in anything dangerous."

"Why didn't you come forward with this information before now, Mr. Taylor?" Carl asked.

"I didn't want to get into trouble. The night Tia left my gym she said that she had a meeting and once that was over with she would be able to come out of hiding." Trevor explained for what seemed like a hundred times.

"My brother just told us today that he and Tia were in a relationship and that she was working hard to turn her life around." Tara added.

"That still doesn't explain why he kept quiet about Ms. Thomas' whereabouts." Carl said.

"I was worried when Tia didn't come back. I knew she wasn't going to contact Tara so when they found her body I was devastated. I loved her and we were planning a life together." Trevor said.

"Do you have any other details to add to this statement, Mr. Taylor?" Carl asked.

"No I don't."

"I'm going to have to send a team to search your gym. Needless to say, Intern Taylor you can't be part of that team." Carl said.

"I want to get to the bottom of this too, Captain. I don't see why I can't be allowed to do my job." Tara said.

"You are not going to talk your way into this search, Intern Taylor. Mr. Taylor, two uniforms and a CSI will escort you to your gym. I'm assuming Ms. Thomas' belongings are still there?"

"Yes, I haven't touched anything in that room she was staying in. I even closed it off from the cleaning crew." Trevor answered.

Carl picked up his phone and requested for the search team. When they were ready, Trey, Trevor, and Jerome went with them. Carl asked Tara to stay.

"Are you sure you don't want to be removed from this case, Intern Taylor?"

"Quite sure, Captain. I need to see this through, not only for Tia but for my brother too." Tara said and Carl told her she was free to leave after asking her a few more questions.

When the group reached the room in the gym that Tia was staying in Trevor told them he would be with them in a minute after he get the key from his office. On his way to his office, Trevor thought over the poor decisions he'd made over the last few months since he was seeing Tia. He lost his better judgment because he wanted to help out someone he came to care a lot about. He knew it would be a long time before Tara would trust him again.

Getting the key out of his locked drawer, Trevor was headed back to join the others when his night manager stopped him. Gary was always calm so when he seemed rattled Trevor became worried. Making a detour and asking his manager to follow him back to his office, Trevor asked Gary what was bothering him.

"Trevor, when I was closing up last night I saw some suspicious characters hanging out on the corner. I didn't think nothing of it until I saw them again when I came in today." Gary said.

"Did they say anything to you?"

"No, they just were standing looking around like they were waiting on someone."

"Thanks for the heads up, Gary. I will check that out. Is there anything else?"

"Well, I was kind of wondering what the police were doing here."

"That is nothing for you to concern about. I'll update you on the situation you just brought to my attention." Trevor told Gary to get back to work while he went to meet the others.

"What took you so long, Trev?" Trey asked.

"I was just talking to my night manager. He said that some suspicious characters were hanging around last night when he closed and today when he came in."

"We will have to talk to him after we finish searching this room." One of the uniform officers said.

Trevor unlocked the door and was shocked to see how messy the room was. He turned on the lights so the officers could get a better view. Tia had clothes thrown all around the room and his laptop she asked to borrow was smashed. Going further into the room, Trevor noticed that the closet door had a lock on it, that he didn't put there.

When he told them he didn't have the key, one of the officers went to the patrol car to get a lock cutter. Cutting off the lock and opening the door the first thing they notice was two large suitcases.

Trevor was baffled because when Tia came to him she didn't have anything with her. He was under the impression that she didn't go anywhere because she was afraid to leave. The clothes that were scattered around he brought for Tia. The officers took the suitcases out of the closet and continued with their search. There was nothing else to the visible eye until they moved further into the closet and saw what looked like a safe. Bringing it out to sit it next to the suitcases, they continued to search. When nothing else was found they attempted to open the suitcases which had locks on them.

Opening the suitcases with the lock cutter the first one contained new designer clothes with the tags still on them. Trevor thought to himself that he really didn't know Tia at all. When the second suitcase was opened everyone was shocked to see money and little white packages that had to be heroin. The officers called Carl who told them not to touch anything else until he and Keshawn arrived. Tara walked in as soon as the officer ended his call with Carl.

"What the hell is all of this?" Tara asked.

"This, my dear sister is what was left here by Tia." Trevor felt like a fool. He knew now that Tia was playing him.

"I don't understand. Why is all of this here?" Tara asked.

"Well, from the looks of it Tia was mixed up and some very shady dealings." Trey said.

"I can't believe this is hers." Tara still didn't want to believe what she saw.

"Well it sure as hell isn't mine." Trevor took a deep breath before continuing. "I guess she was playing both of us, Tara.

"Trey, what did you find out about, Tia?" Tara asked.

"Well, that night when her body was found, I went home and did some digging. It seems that Tia was involved with running drugs and the merchandise here."

"Why would she do this? She had a good job and was talking about going back to school?" Tara said.

"Tara, Tia got fired from her job two weeks before her disappearance." Jerome added.

"Why didn't you guys tell me what was going on. How was I supposed to help her if I didn't know she was in trouble? This has Tameka written all over it." Tara insisted.

"I'm sure Carl will take that into consideration, but you have to accept that Tia wasn't as innocent as you wanted her to be." Trey said.

"I need some air. Excuse me." Tara left and went outside to clear her head.

"She played me big time. She had all this illegal shit in my gym and didn't bat an eye that she was putting all of us at risk." Trevor said.

"Calm down, man. You are not the first guy to get taken in by a pretty face." Jerome said.

"And you won't be the last, Trev. Let's wait to see what's next when Carl and Keshawn arrives." Trey added.

"I'll be in my office." Trevor left the room and headed to his office. He wanted to cry but knew that wouldn't get him anywhere.

Chapter Eight

Tara sat in her bedroom at her parents' house the morning after Trevor's gym was searched. She couldn't believe how things spiraled out of control so quickly. Carl and Keshawn arrived and took everything that was in Trevor's locked room down for evidenced. She didn't feel like driving so Trey offered to take her home. Jerome followed them driving her car.

Walking her to her door, they were about to say goodbye until they noticed her door was cracked opened. Pulling out their guns the trio slowly proceeded into Tara's apartment. The entryway was the only part of the placed that wasn't disturbed. Each room they went into was worse than the one before. When Tara walked into her bedroom her mattress was flipped over to the other side of the room. Clothes were thrown everywhere. She didn't wait around to check out anything else. The trio left called in the disturbance and took Tara to Trenton and Tanya's house.

Tara cried for the friend she thought she knew. Was Tia just playing her all along? What was the purpose of her getting involved with Trevor? She had to know that would have bothered Tara. What was Tameka's part in all of this? Tara had so many questions with no answers. She wished she could be with Keshawn right now, but she didn't like him to come around her parent's house because they didn't like him. Trey was like that at first too, but he seemed to be more accepting now. Tara hoped her parents would come around soon.

Tara decided until she gets proof that Tia was up to no good with her and Trevor, she was going to give Tia the benefit of doubt. This wasn't going to sit well with her parents, but she had to do what was right in her heart. It did scare her that someone would destroy her apartment, but they would get to the bottom of that too. Trey was going to pick her up so they could head to the office. Tara was so out of it she didn't realize Trey and Jerome was having her followed. They both regretted they didn't have her apartment under surveillance, if they did they would have known who trashed it.

The firm should have the reports on Tameka and Tony within the next day or two. Tara now felt both were involved in Tia's death. The clothing found at Trevor's gym had Tameka's name written all over it. The drugs had to be Tony's. Tara still didn't feel that Tia was using her, but Tia got mixed up in something that was over her head. Thinking about it now, Tia's behavior had changed somewhat over the last year, but Tara had put it down to the turmoil Tony was taking her through.

Tara hoped she didn't have to go through another family meeting anytime soon. She was waiting on Talia to get there so they could work on their relationship. The girls knew their parents were at their wits end with the two of them not getting along. Their mom was at work and their dad was out working on something with TJ, so this was the perfect time for the two of them to meet. As soon as Tara finished dressing and went into the kitchen she heard Talia entering the house.

"Good morning, Tara." Talia said.

"Good morning, Talia, how are you doing this morning?" Tara responded.

"I guess that would depend on how our conversation goes. Mom is right. We need to learn how to co-exist."

"I have no problem with that, but you have to realize I have my own mind and stop treating me like a bothersome child." Tara thought for a moment. "I know I need to make some changes too, especially where Linda is concerned."

"That's a big start, Tara. I know Trey means a lot to you, but he is important to all of us."

"I guess I expected Linda to be more supportive of Trey and to have his back. I mean if Ronnie (Talia's husband) was in a similar situation, wouldn't you stand by him?" Tara asked.

"Yes, I would, but Linda was pregnant at the time, so her hormones were all out of whack." Talia explained.

"I know the family may not believe me, but my feelings of possessiveness towards Trey have changed since my relationship with Keshawn."

"That's good. I will do my best to stop treating you like a child and be a bit more objective about your feelings. It's just hard, since you're the youngest everyone wants to baby you all the time."

"I'm glad we had this talk, Talia. I need my big sister now that I find out more disturbing information about Tia." Tara said. The sisters hugged and chatted until it was time for Talia to go to work.

Tara, Trey, and Jerome were working in the conference room later that morning after Trey picked Tara up. Before they got started Tara told the guys about her meeting with Talia that morning. She also told them that she was going to work harder at building a relationship with Linda. The trio worked for a few hours more until Tara's cell phone rang. Seeing that it was, Carl, Tara answered right away.

"Good afternoon, Captain."

"Intern Taylor, I need to see you in my office right away." Carl said.

"Is there new information in Tia's case?" Tara asked.

"We'll talk about that when you get here."

"Okay, I was working with Trey and Jerome. Is it okay if they come with me?"

Pausing for a moment, Carl said, "Why not, we will just have a party over here. Yes, its fine, just get here right away please." Carl said before disconnecting the call.

"Captain wants me to come to his office right away. I got permission for you guys to come too."

"Did Carl say it was about Tia's case?" Trey asked.

"He wouldn't say, but I think there have been new developments by the sound of his voice." Tara responded as the trio headed out to the police station.

Chapter Nine

The trio arrived at the police station half hour after Carl's call. On the drive over they discuss the different scenarios that may have come up since the police collected the evidence from Trevor's gym. Trey who was down on Carl most of the time told the crew that Carl was a good leader and motivator even though he was a by the book guy. Now as the trio was sitting in front of Carl's desk, Carl started the conversation.

Intern Taylor it seems as though Ms. Thomas was in the process of assuming your identity." Carl said.

"No disrespect, Sir, I don't think Tia would do that to me." Tara said.

"We'll there is evidence that says differently." Carl responded.

"What kind of evidence, Carl." Trey asked.

"We finally finished cataloging the items from the search of your brother's gym. We found a driver's license, several credit cards, passport, and a social security card. Tia's picture was on the driver license and passport, but all the information listed as being you, Intern Taylor." Carl explained.

"This is unreal. Something else has to be going on here, Captain." Tara said.

"Why are you finding it so difficult to believe that your friend was up to no good, Intern Taylor?" Carl asked.

"Tia could have gotten anything she wanted from me. She was my best friend. I would have known if she had an axe to grind against me." Tara insisted.

"If that was the case, how can you explain the evidence we found in her possession?" Carl asked.

"I will not rush to judgment, Captain. This is all too neat just like the case against Trey years ago." Tara insisted.

"Tara you may have to accept the fact that Tia wasn't really your friend." Jerome said.

"The only thing I have to accept is that there is a lot we don't know about this case. Until all the facts are in, I'm not going to persecute Tia." Tara said and left the room before they could see the tears forming in her eyes.

"Carl, what else was found?" Trey asked.

"You know I can't divulge that information to you, Trey. You need to prepare your sister because all the evidence points to the fact that Ms. Thomas was just using her."

"I have my sister and brother's back, Carl. I have mixed feelings about this situation, but we know that Tara has great instincts. If she feels this deeply about something else is going on, than we have to dig deeper." Trey responded.

"Trey, not we, the department will take care of this situation. You need to convince your sister to leave this case alone, especially after what happened at her apartment."

"Tara is going to see this case through no matter what the danger. If she wouldn't back down when my dad ordered her to, then we just have to make sure she doesn't get in over her head."

"She's already in over her head." Carl stood. "Talk to her again please. You know I can have her removed from this case, but what she does from there if I do remove her is on you guys." Carl walked Trey and Jerome to the door saying he had a meeting to attend.

When Time Runs Out: Tara's Quest for Vengeance

Tara was sitting in the police station lobby waiting on Trey and Jerome to finish up with Carl. She was so deep in her thoughts that at first she didn't pay attention to her vibrating phone. Looking down at unavailable across her screen, Tara started not to answer, but she thought it may have something to do with Tia's case.

"This is Tara."

"You better watch your back."

"Who is this?" Tara asked but the call was disconnected.

Tara thought to herself, *"Now the games begin."* Just then Trey and Jerome came out and told her they needed to get back to the office. Tara waited until they were seated in the conference room before she told them about the call.

"Tara, why didn't you mention this at the police station?" Trey asked.

"Because, I didn't think it was a big deal."

"Right now everything is a big deal since we are not sure what is going on." Jerome added.

"I don't need the two of you gaining up on me." Tara said pouting.

"We'll deal with that later. Right now we have our work cut out for us checking into this identity thing." Trey said.

"Let's do that. While I was waiting on you guys to finish up with the Captain, I checked my bank accounts, put a fraud alert on my credit report, changed my passwords, and was going to check the utilities company when we're done." Tara explained.

"I'm glad you jumped right on this, Tara. I know this is difficult for you." Trey said.

"We still have a lot to process, but as I said I will not believe this is Tia's handy work at this point."

"Tara, you may have to consider this as an option. Who else would have enough information on you beside family to have all those documents made?" Trey asked.

"I don't know, Trey. Could you just take me to Mom and Dad's? I need time to think."

"Sure, Jerome could you start a file on this identity thing? I will come straight back, after I drop Tara off."

"I also order my credit reports. I will print them off tonight so we can add that to the file." Tara and Trey left the office and headed to their parents' house.

<u>Chapter Ten</u>

The next morning Tara woke up early. She didn't sleep well last night. She missed her apartment and Keshawn. Talking to him over the phone wasn't enough. Tia had been heavy on her mind. In her heart she knew that Tia didn't play her or Trevor, but her head was telling her to keep an open mind. Thinking about Tia, Tara thought about the time when they first met in middle school.

"This is my seat you're sitting in." Tara said to the beautiful girl.

"We don't have assigned seating in here." The girl responded.

"I know you've seen me sitting in this seat since the semester started."

"Listen, I got a headache so go away and leave me alone."

"Just get up out of my seat, chic" Tara said.

"I know you didn't just call me a chic, heifer?" The girl said.

"I sure did." Tara responded as she proceeded to pull on the girl's arm to make her get up. The next thing they knew, they were sent to the office for fighting. Once they were there, and their parents were called, the assistant principal asked the girls to explain what happened again.

"This rude girl started a fight with me saying I was sitting in her seat" The girl answered.

"My name is Tara and you better watch your mouth." Tara warned.

"That's enough, Tara." The assistant principal said. "Why must you always make trouble?"

"I wasn't making trouble. I just wanted to have a seat so I could finish up my work." Tara said.

"Tia, I expect you girls to work this out. I couldn't reach your mom, so you're going to have to stay here until I do. As for you, Tara, your mom couldn't get off work so your brother will be picking you up."

"Good, Trey will not like you guys picking on me." Tara said.

"Trey isn't picking you up, Tara. TJ will be picking you up." The assistant principal said. She knew the entire Taylor family very well.

Tara's face dropped. "Why did you call him? I'm sure he is busy in court." Tara didn't want to hear TJ's lecture.

"I called him because that is what your mom suggested. Now, have you girls introduced yourselves? Tara, this is Tia Thomas, she is new to our school. Tia this is Tara Taylor."

The girls looked at each other but didn't say a word so the assistant principal continued, "You guys have a lot in common, both of you are taking honor courses."

"When my brother gets here, you need to tell him that she started this mess. I don't feel like hearing his lecture today." Tara said.

"My name is Tia. I didn't start anything. We don't have assigned seating. If you had just sat somewhere else none of this would have happened." Tia responded.

"Don't talk to me." Tara said as TJ walked into the office with a frustrated look on his face.

The knock on Tara's door brought her back to the present. "Come in."

"Good morning, Tara." Trenton said.

"Good morning, Dad."

"After you get dressed, I need you to come to the family room."

"Sure, Dad, give me fifteen minutes." Trenton left Tara's room and she rushed to get dressed.

When Tara walked into the family room, she was surprised to see Trey, Jerome, and another man she didn't know. She entered and sat next to Trey and Jerome. Trenton sat across from them with a frown on his face. Before she could asked what was going on Trenton spoke.

"Tara this is a buddy of mine, Mark. He has interesting information to share."

"Good morning, Tara. Your dad had me doing a little research on a few people in your inner circle, especially your deceased friend Tia Thomas."

"Dad, why didn't you let us know what you were doing? We need to work together so we won't be covering the same bases."

"Tara, I think you need to listen closely to what Mark uncovered." Trenton said.

"This goes back more than twenty years. It seems the lady that is passing herself off as Tameka Thomas is a fraud. Tameka Thomas has been deceased since nineteen ninety-six, one month after giving birth to Tia. Cause of death was complications from the delivery"

"Wow, so who is the lady that is claiming to be Tia's mom?" Tara asked. She was shocked by this information.

"Jackie Brown, she was the best friend of Tameka Thomas. Ms. Thomas was Tia Thomas' biological mom. Ms. Brown assumed Tameka Thomas' identity when she passed away." Mark said.

"So that woman is no relation to, Tia? I knew it was something off about her." Tara said.

"There is an APB out for Ms. Brown." Mark said.

"I was wondering why I haven't heard from her. Tia's funeral is this Saturday. She was supposed to get back with me by now for the money she said she needed for incidentals." Tara explained.

"I guess we didn't dig deep enough when we did our background check." Trey added.

"Here is the kicker. It seems that Anthony Brown (Tony) is the younger brother of Jackie Brown."

"So that is why that woman always took his side over Tia's. I can't believe this crazy mess." Tara thought for a moment. "Wait a minute. Will Tony be picked up for questioning too?"

"Not on this matter." Mark answered.

"Trey, we have to go see the Captain. This puts a new light on the case. We have to be there when they bring that imposter in." Tara said.

"There are additional details in this report that may help you guys." Mark said handing Trey the report.

"Thank you, Mark and Dad. We have to go take this information to the police station." Tara said. She gave her dad a brief hug and shook Mark's hand before the trio headed out to the police station. She didn't stay long enough for them to let her know that the police was aware of the new findings.

<u>Chapter Eleven</u>

Tara was anxious on the drive over to the police station. She was quiet, trying to get her thoughts straight. So it was finally coming into place why Jackie was so distant from Tia and always taking Tony's side. She wished she had asked how Tia's biological mom died. Maybe it was in the report Mark gave to Trey. She wouldn't put it pass Jackie to have something to do with it. Unfortunately, Tony was too young so that situation couldn't be blamed on him. Once they arrived and was shown to Carl's office, Tara started to explain right away.

"Captain, my dad had Tameka and Tony investigated and you're not going to believe what he came up with."

"Let me save you some time, Intern Taylor. It has been brought to our attention already that Tameka Thomas died years ago shortly have giving birth to Tia Thomas."

"So when did you find this out, Captain." Tara asked.

"I found out last night, when your dad's investigator sent over his findings. Before you ask, your dad said they would take care of updating you." Carl said.

"So has Jackie Brown been apprehended yet?" Trey asked.

"No, the search is still on for Ms. Brown and her brother Tony."

"So you will be bringing Tony in for questioning? My dad's investigator said that he couldn't be brought in for this issue." Tara said.

"No, Mr. Brown's arrest warrant doesn't have anything to do with Ms. Brown's fraud or Ms. Thomas murder case." Carl explained.

"Then, why is he being brought in, Captain Marshall." Jerome asked.

"That is classified information. What I can tell you guys if things pan out Mr. Brown would be a senior citizen before he walks the streets again if he ever gets out." Before Carl could say anything else Keshawn knocked briefly on the door and walked in once he was given permission.

"Captain, we have the suspect waiting in Interrogation Room 2." Keshawn said.

Before Carl could answer Tara asked, "Is it the imposter or her no good brother?"

"Intern Taylor that's enough, Detective Konner, I'll meet you in there in a few minutes." Carl said. After Keshawn left he turned to Tara, "That is exactly what I'm talking about. You are too emotionally involved in this case, Intern Taylor."

"I just asked one simple question, Captain."

"It's not your place to ask questions. You're working the crime scene only. Is that clear?"

"Yes, Sir it's crystal clear." Tara said.

"Now if you guys excuse me, I need to take care of this situation. I will keep you guys posted." Carl walked the trio to the lobby door and headed towards the Interrogation Room.

"I think we need to stick around. I want to know what that woman has to say for herself." Tara said.

"No, baby girl, we need to get back to the office and let the police do their jobs. Besides we have plenty of work to keep us busy with the new information Mark gathered." Trey said.

"Okay, but we better get some answers soon and closed this case. I'm ready to go back to my apartment." Tara said. As the trio walked to the car, they were unaware they were being watched.

Trey droved a few blocks away from the police station and notice they were being followed. He didn't want to alert Tara. She was in the back seat fussing that Carl was getting on her last nerve. Getting Jerome attention by their secret signal both men was on alert now. Trey knew he had to think quickly. He didn't want to lead his followers to his office, but deviating would get Tara's attention. Knowing he didn't have any choice he had to let Tara know what was going on.

"Tara, I need you to lie down back there."

"What's going on, Trey?" Tara asked.

"We have been followed since we left the police station?" Jerome explained.

"Why didn't you guys tell me?" Tara asked while doing as Trey asked. She reached down to retrieve her revolver from her leg holster.

The next events happened quickly. First they were rear-ended, then a dark car with tinted windows moved along the side of them and started shooting. Trey speeded up and then hit his brakes quickly. The car moved forward and now Trey was driving behind the car that didn't have a license plate. Jerome was mad because he had taken his phone out to try to get the license plate number. Following the car a few more blocks, the trio was shocked to see the car spiraling out of control hitting a yield sign before flipping over and coming to a stop. There were police sirens in the background. Trey decided not to get any closer to the car and let the police handle the situation.

Tara jumped out of the car before Trey or Jerome could stop her. She was headed to the stalled car as a man slid from underneath. Trey and Jerome jumped out and pushed Tara out of the way. Next all you could hear was gun fire. The police had arrived and shot the assailant, but not before Jerome and Tara watched as Trey laid on the ground unconscious.

They ran over to Trey as they heard the EMS getting closer. Trey was bleeding from the front of his shirt after they opened his jacket. Tara took her scarf off and applied pressure to his wounds. A few minutes later the EMS asked them to give them room so they could work on Trey. Once they had him on the stretcher and in the back of their vehicle, Tara asked Jerome to call the family while she went with Trey to the hospital.

<u>Chapter Twelve</u>

Most of the Taylor family was at the hospital awaiting word of Trey's condition. Jerome was able to contact all the family except for TJ who was tied up in court and Trevor. He left several messages for Trevor with no response. The hardest call he had to make was to Linda so instead of making the call he went over to her house and picked her up. They were in luck that Linda's baby sister was there visiting and she was able to stay with the baby.

Trey's mom and sister Talia were already at the hospital since both of them were on duty. When Jerome walked in with Linda, Tara who was still covered in Trey's blood was there with Trenton. About an hour after Jerome arrived at the hospital with Linda, TJ showed up. The family was worried because they still didn't hear any word from Trevor. Linda was sympathetic towards Tara until she found out how Trey had gotten hurt.

"Little girl, what is it going to take for you to think about someone else besides yourself? Trey has put his life on the line too many times for you." Linda said through her tears.

"Everything happened so fast. I was just trying to find out who was in the car that shot at us." Tara explained, still in shock.

"If Trey and Jerome stayed in the car to wait for the police, why couldn't you do the same? The only thing that is important to you is getting your way. You better hope my husband pull through this."

"That's enough, Linda. This situation could happen at any time in Trey's line of work." Trenton scolded his daughter-in-law.

"I know that, Mr. Trent, but all she had to do is stay her behind in the car and wait for the police." Linda said with tears still falling down her face.

"Linda this isn't Tara's fault. You need to calm down and pray for TT's recovery." Jerome.

"Things have to change. I'm not going to tell my son his dad won't be home because his auntie is too damn selfish to put anybody needs before her own."

"I had enough of you. Trey is the most important person in my life. I would never do anything to put him in danger." Tara stood, walked over, and got in Linda's face.

"I won't have any more discussion about this. Both of you sit your asses down and don't say another word." Trenton said. A few minutes later Tanya, Talia, another nurse and doctor came into the waiting room. The Dr. Gordon went straight to Linda to let her know Trey's condition.

"Mrs. Taylor you can see Trey as soon as he is moved from recovery to his room. At his point he is in stable condition. He is in and out of consciousness, but he kept asking for Tara. To put his mind at ease it may be a good idea for her to visit him first so he can be assured she is okay." The doctor knew the Taylor family well.

"That's not going to happen. She is the reason he is hurt in the first place." Linda said angrily.

Talia walked over to her best friend. "That is not true, Linda. Trey needs to see Tara first so he can rest peacefully."

"Why are you taking her side, Lia when you know that she is responsible?" Linda was the only one that shorten Talia's name.

"Thank you Dr. Gordon. Let us know when Tara can see Trey." Trenton said. "Linda, you need to get your emotions in check and make sure my son needs are met." The doctor and nurse left the family. Tanya and Trenton went out to get some air.

After her parents left, Tara walked over to Linda, "I'm so sorry, Linda, please forgive me." Tara said and left to go to the ladies room.

Trevor sat in the dark room that he had been in for the last few days. He knew he should have kept in touch with the family, but he was out of sorts with Tia's death. His emotions went for sadness to anger to sympathy. He had to find a way to come to grips with what his life has become over the last few months since getting involved with Tia. He couldn't believe that he fallen in love with someone so young and especially someone with all of Tia's issues.

He had several calls from the family that he hadn't returned. He was embarrassed to face them right now, especially Tara. He loved his baby sister and didn't like disappointing her. He knew it was time for him to stop feeling sorry for himself. His thoughts were interrupted when he heard his phone vibrate. Looking at the message from his dad only saying 911, Trevor knew his moments of alone time had ended. Calling his dad's phone he was ready for his dad's anger.

"Hey, dad, what's up? Trevor tried to sound normal.

"Get over to the hospital right away. Trey has been injured."

"Is he okay?"

"He is in stable condition right now, but he took two bullets to the stomach." Trenton said.

"Oh my God, I will be over right away. How are Mom and the rest of the family holding up?"

"We're all at the hospital right now. We'll update you when you get here."

"Okay, I will be there in about twenty minutes." Trevor ended the call, took a quick shower, and headed to the hospital.

<u>Chapter Thirteen</u>

It was now Friday afternoon and all the family was at Trey and Linda's house to welcome him home from the hospital. The doctor would have liked to keep Trey for a few more days, but Trey said he had to get out of there so he could attend Tia's funeral the next day. Tanya and Talia assured the doctor they would keep an eye on Trey. Linda and Tara still weren't friendly towards each other, but decided to put their differences aside for Trey's sake. Linda was upset when Tara asked for everyone attention to make an announcement.

"In light of recent events and Tony's arrest for the car incident I've decided to step away for Tia's murder case." Tara said.

Rolling her eyes at Tara, Linda responded, "A little late for that move."

"Linda not now, you sure you want to leave this case unsolved, baby girl?" Trey asked.

"Yes, I'm very sure, Trey. I think eventually they will find that Tony was somehow involved. Plus since Jackie has been put behind bars, two of the people that made Tia's life miserable are out of commission." Tara answered.

"Well, you do realize Tia's case is still open and until they find out what happened to her, your life is still in danger?" Jerome said.

"Yes, I realize that Jerome, but I have faith that the police will solve this case soon, and I'll be able to return home."

"Tara there is still a lot of unanswered questions. Tia's was connected to some shady characters. I don't think you or Trev is safe." TJ added.

"I'll be okay. I've been extra careful and added additional security at the gym." Trevor said.

"I got a feeling in my gut that the funeral tomorrow will be a turning point in the case." Trenton said.

"Why do you say that, Dad?" Trey asked.

"Well, from the information gathered so far we know that Jackie and Tony are not the brains of the operation. Since neither one of them is talking we still have to be on alert for anything that may occur. For the reason alone, Trey, you should not attend the funeral."

"Come on, Dad. I may not be one hundred percent, but I can still take care of myself. Besides JW will be with me and so will the rest of you guys."

"I agree with your dad, Trey. You should stay here to recuperate since you left the hospital against the doctor's order." Linda said.

"I appreciate all of you coming over, but I'm kind of tired. I will rest for the remainder of the day. I'm sure I will feel much stronger tomorrow." Trey said. He asked Linda to see everyone out before headed off to take a nap.

Tara was in her room at her parents' house. She was too restless to sleep. She blamed herself for Trey getting hurt. *Why didn't I just stay in the car until the police arrived?* She knew Linda was right. She had to accept responsibility and stop holding the family hostage to her whelms. Still missing Tia, Tara went back to the time after they got into trouble for fighting.

"I think it's time to squash our differences, Tia." Tara said to *the girl who was sitting alone at the table in the lunchroom.*

"What do you have up your sleeve now, Tara?" Tia asked.

"Nothing, I just see you eating alone every day and you don't seem to have any friends."

"I don't but that is by choice." Tia answered.

"Why do you have to be so mean when all I'm trying to do is make conversation with you?"

"I enjoy my own company, so I don't have a need to make friends." Tia said.

"Well, I tried. If you change your mind let me know." Tara said and left the girl to her own devices. Later that afternoon Tia approached Tara to apologize for being rude. Since that day they were best friends. Tara learned that Tia was living with her single mom and was at the school on special scholarships because of her academic achievements.

Tia had a strong personality that should have clashed with Tara's but it didn't. The two girls got along famously. They took many of their classes together. The main differences between the girls were that Tia seemed to look for love in the wrong places and Tara wasn't into boys yet. Most of the time Tia was interested in older men, but Tara equated that to her not having a male presence in her life. Tara thought about the time when Tia told her about her relationship with Tony.

"Tara, I think he is the one. You should be happy that I'm interested in someone in our age group."

"I want more than that for you. I heard some bad things about Tony, Tia."

"You know how people blow things out of proportion on the streets."

"Just be careful." Tara said. One year into their relationship Tony started hitting Tia and Tara think he was also passing Tia around to his friends, but Tia always denied that claim. It took Tia another two years to finally end the relationship. Going back to her old ways of dating older men Trevor was the answered for Tia. Coming out of her thoughts when her cell phone rang with an unfamiliar number, Tara answered cautiously. When the operator told her she had a collect call from Cook County Sheriff Department Tara started to hang up since she knew it was Jackie, but she went ahead and stayed on the phone.

"What the hell do you want, Jackie?" Tara asked.

"You can stop with the attitude." Jackie said.

"State what you want or I'm hanging up."

"How would you like to find out what happened to Tia?" Jackie asked.

"I'm off the case. Any information you have you need to pass along to the police."

"Not this information. I think you better start taking me seriously, little girl."

"I'm not a little girl and I don't have anything else to say to you." Tara was about to end the call when she heard Jackie yell.

"I know who murdered, Tia."

"Tell the police."

"I don't think you want me to do that, Tara."

"I don't have time for your games, Jackie. I have to bury my best friend tomorrow."

"This is your last chance. You better come to see me first thing in the morning. If you don't your family will never be the same." Jackie ended the call before Tara could say anything else.

<u>Chapter Fourteen</u>

Early the next morning before getting ready for the funeral, Tara called Jerome and asked him to meet her at the office. She asked him not to tell Trey they were meeting. She had another restless night after talking to Jackie. At first Tara didn't know what to do. At a time like this she usually turned to Trey for help, but since that wasn't an option she called Jerome. Now sitting in the conference room with Jerome, Tara got started. She told him about Jackie's call and informed him that she asked Trevor to join them.

"What do you think this mean, Jerome? It seemed to me that Jackie was hinting at Trevor being involved in Tia's murder."

"Who knows what is going on in that crazy woman's mind? You can't go see her alone, Tara." Jerome said.

"I know, that is why I called you and Trev. I want you guys to go with me."

"Wait a minute. If she is going to implicate Trev, she is not going to talk to you in front of him."

"I thought of that too, but Trev has a right to defend himself if Jackie starts slinging accusations"

"That's understandable, but if she doesn't talk to us because Trev is there then it would be a wasted trip." Jerome explained as Trevor walked in the door.

"Morning, Trev. Sorry to get you out so early, but I received a call from Jackie and she said that she knows who murdered Tia. She also said that if I didn't come see her this morning it would mean big trouble for our family." Tara said.

"I know you aren't planning on going to see her, Tara." Trevor said.

"Yes, we all are. We need to get this taken care of so we can get ready for the funeral." Tara answered.

"I told, Tara that if she is on the right track and Jackie is planning on implicating you, then she won't talk to us if you are there." Jerome said.

"He's right, Tara. Jackie isn't going to talk if I'm there." Trevor said.

"Trev, is there something that you need to tell us? You have this uneasy look on your face." Tara asked.

"Tara, I know you're not asking me if I'm involved in Tia's murder." Trevor said.

"No, big brother, I'm not asking you that, but I need to know if there is something that you haven't shared with us about Tia."

"Tara now is not the time to talk about this." Trevor said.

Trevor's comment made Tara uncomfortable. "Trev, you need to let us know right now if you are holding anything back. You know we will have your back." Tara said.

"Tara is right, Trev, we got your back, but you have to come clean with us if you want our help." Jerome added.

"There is one detail I left out and since I waited so long I didn't know what to do about it." Trevor said.

"What detail was that, Trev?" Tara asked.

"Well, the morning after the last time I saw Tia, someone had pried their way through the first door at the gym. I think when they figured out they couldn't go any further they left, but not before leaving me a little present."

"What did they leave you, Trev?" Jerome asked.

Silent tears rolled down Trevor face, "It was the clothes that Tia's was wearing the last time I saw her and they were bloody." Trevor said.

"Oh my God, Trev, what did you do with them?" Tara asked.

"I panic and didn't know what to do with them so I hid them in my safe." Trevor explained.

"Why didn't you take them to the police?" Tara asked.

"Because I was afraid they were going to think I did something to Tia. I had already made the mistake of hiding her. I guess whoever killed her made her tell them where she had been hiding so they could get to the money, clothes, and drugs."

"Trev we have to go to the police." Jerome said.

"I know, but I just want to get through Tia's funeral, then I will turn myself in."

"I knew Jackie had something to do with all of this. She knows you are in possession of those clothes so she is going to try to use that to force our hand."

"Man, I wish TT was here. He would know exactly how to handle this situation." Jerome said.

"Well, we can't involve Trey right now. What we need to do is go to the funeral and afterwards get the clothes and take them to the police." Tara said.

"I'm so sorry guys. I've been going out of my mind with losing Tia and the thought of getting blamed for what happened to her..."

"Trev, you should have told us this when it happened. Now you gave the police reason to believe you were involved." Tara said.

"I know. I started telling TJ about what was going on, but he said as an officer of the court that I shouldn't tell him anything that may come back to bite me."

"Why wouldn't you come to one of us, Trev?" Tara asked.

"Because I knew you were still mad at me and I didn't want to put Trey and Jerome in an uncomfortable position."

"Well, let's get out of here. We can't go to the repast. I will make up an excuse for the family. Jerome and I will go with you. We can't let Trey get involved, he is not strong enough." Tara said. They all agreed and headed out to get ready for the funeral.

<u>Chapter Fifteen</u>

The church was crowed. The Pastor had just finished the service and the men lined up to get ready to carry Tia's body out to the hearse. TJ, Trevor, and Jerome were on one side of the casket while three of Tara and Tia's high school friends were on the other side. Trey was upset that he was not strong enough to help. He sat in the front row with Linda who was still upset that she was not able to talk him out of attending.

Tara glanced at Trevor often to see how he was holding up. With the evidence they had to turn in, she had the feeling that Trevor was in big trouble. She wished Keshawn was there, but he couldn't get off work. The repast was going to be at her parent's house. She had already made excuses to her parents about why the three of them would be late. She told them not to tell Trey they were going to be late so he wouldn't ask them a thousand and one questions.

As the men made it out to the hearse and put the casket inside, Tara noticed Carl and Keshawn was hanging around in the back of the crowd. She also noticed the panic look on Trevor's face when he saw them. To keep everything normal Tara rushed over to Carl and

Keshawn and asked them to meet her back inside the church since it was now empty.

"What are you guys doing here?" Tara asked.

"New details have come up in the case and we need to talk to your brother."

Pretending he was talking about, Trey, Tara said, "Captain, Trey is still weak. Can he come down to the station within the next day or two?"

"We're not here for, Trey, Intern Taylor, but for your brother, Trevor." Carl said.

"Trevor, what do you want with him, Captain?"

"That's enough stalling, Intern Taylor. We come to take Trevor in for questioning." Carl said.

"Captain, you know my family. Please don't make a scene. I promise to have Trevor at the station within the hour." Tara said.

"Captain, I will stay here with the family and make sure Tara keeps her word." Keshawn said.

"Ok, Konner, I expect to see him in my office within the hour." Carl said and left the church.

Tara hugged Keshawn and thanked him over and over. A few minutes later Jerome and Trevor walked into the church.

"The family is gone. I guess this isn't a social visit?" Trevor said to Keshawn.

"No, man, I'm sorry it's not. I have to escort you to the police station." Keshawn answered.

"Thank you for not making a scene. We would have been in here earlier, but Trey kept asking tons of questions." Trevor explained.

"I understand and I'm sorry it has to come to this." Keshawn pulled out his handcuffs.

"No, baby you can't do that." Tara said now sobbing.

Keshawn was torn, but knew that Trevor wasn't going to make a run for it, so he asked Jerome to drive and Tara to sit in the front of the car with him while he and Trevor sat in the back.

When they arrived at the police station, Tara told Trevor not to say anything until they were able to reach Victoria. She was not able to reach Victoria so she had to do the next best thing: contact her dad. He was going to be boiling mad but that was the chance she had to take. She and Jerome still felt it was best not to involve Trey right now. Getting her dad on the phone, Tara told him the situation.

"I knew something wasn't right. Why the hell you let this happen, Tara without informing me?" Trenton asked.

"Dad, we didn't want to disrupt the funeral." Tara explained.

"To hell with the funeral, my son is in trouble and you didn't see fit to tell me."

"We didn't want Trey to get involved right now, he isn't strong enough." Tara explained.

"Victoria and I will be down as soon as possible. Make sure Trevor doesn't make a statement, even to your boyfriend." Trenton said.

Tara didn't like the way her dad tried not to never mention Keshawn by name, but she had bigger fish to fry. "I already told him that, Dad."

"I will let your mom know what is going on. She will keep it under wraps for now."

Thank you, Dad. See you guys soon." Tara ended her call and turned to face Jerome.

"Jerome, I don't think we are going to be able to hide this from Trey. When dad and Victoria get here, I think we better go over to Trey's house and give him an update. My dad said he went home after the funeral."

"I know, but TT is going to let us have it. He doesn't like to be kept in the dark." Jerome said.

"I know and it's not going to help that we have to deal with Linda. I know she doesn't want Trey to get involved. She is not going to be happy to see me."

"She'll be okay, Tara. She just wants to keep Trey safe."

"She can't do that. In his line of work this is bound to happen so she has to toughen up and accept the fact that Trey thrives on this kind of excitement."

"Tara, you need to lighten up on Linda. Don't you remember promising to work things out with her after you and Talia made up?"

"Yes, I did, but you saw how she attacked me at the hospital. She just wants Trey all to herself when he has a family that loves him just as much as she does."

"Tara, I think it's time for someone to talk to you about your relationship with Trey. He is always going to love you and be there for you, but you need to cut him some slack. You put him in a bad position when you don't get along with Linda." Jerome said.

"I know. I don't ever want to put Trey in the position of choosing between me and Linda. I know you see how I let go of him somewhat when I became serious about Keshawn."

"I did see it and so did Trey. I think he was a little jealous for a while because he was used to having you to himself."

"I promised to deal with Linda for Trey's sake, but I don't ever see us becoming close because she is too weak to deal with Trey's personality and work."

"Linda is stronger than you think, Tara. Give her a chance. Your family is hard to deal with at times."

"Okay, let's talk about something else until dad and Victoria gets here." Tara and Jerome continued to make small talk until the others arrived.

<u>Chapter Sixteen</u>

Tara and Jerome pulled up to Trey's house later that afternoon. They knew Trevor was in good hands with Trenton and Victoria. They dreaded telling Trey what was going on. Of course Linda didn't want them to come over saying Trey was just getting up from a nap after the funeral. Linda led them into the den where Trey was sitting in his favorite recliner reading the newspaper.

"Hey, guys. Glad you stopped by?" Trey said in a good mood.

"Hi, Trey, how are you feeling?" Tara asked.

"Much better after my nap, I guess I was a little tired after the funeral."

"Hey, TT, that is what we're here to talk to you about." Jerome said.

"Okay, I'm all ears, what going on?" Trey asked.

"Well, Trey after the funeral, the Captain and Keshawn came by to take Trev in for questioning in Tia's case." Tara said.

"Why didn't you guys tell me before I left the church? Where is Trev now?" Trey asked becoming frustrated.

"He's at the police station with your dad and Victoria." Jerome answered.

"JW, I can't believe you guys didn't let me know what was going on. This is my company in case both of you have forgotten." Trey said angrily.

"Listen, Trey. All of this went down this morning after I received a call from Jackie last night demanding I come see her first thing this morning."

"Linda, please come in here right now." Trey yelled. When Malinda entered the room Trey said, "Let me make this perfectly clear now that we all are together. If anything important pertaining to my business or to my family arises, I expect to be told immediately. I know my limits better than anyone, is that clear?"

"Calm down, Trey. I'm not going to let you make me feel guilty for protecting you. You should still be in the hospital." Linda defended herself.

"I don't need you or anyone else telling me what I need. Tara, Jerome, I'm going to change and you guys are going to drive me over to the police station." Trey left the room.

"Why did you guys have to tell him this mess? He shouldn't be out in the field, but here resting." Linda said.

"You see how upset he is now, Linda. If we had waited any longer he would have really hit the roof." Jerome said.

"That's beside the point." Linda said turning to Tara, "The best thing for this family is for you to just go away."

"No the best thing for this family is for Trey to get a wife that has the guts to stand by him in good and bad times." Tara responded.

"Ladies, stop all of this nonsense before TT comes back in here." Jerome said.

"Find with me, I'll be in the car." Tara left Jerome and Linda in the den and headed for the car.

By the time Trey, Tara, and Jerome arrived at the police station, Trevor had already been released but was in the conference room with Carl, Trenton, and Victoria. The trio was escorted into the conference room. Trevor looked exhausted and now he was in the same boat as Tara, banished to go home with their dad for legal and safety purposes. Trenton order extra security for his house, Trey's house, and Trey's PI firm. Carl left the room so the family could discuss the details of Trevor's questioning.

"What the hell are you doing here, Trey? I told you guys not to bring him down here." Trenton yelled at Tara and Jerome.

"They didn't have a choice. If they didn't bring me, I do know how to drive myself, Dad." Trey said.

"Don't get smart with me, boy. You know you should be at home resting. We got this handled."

Ignoring his dad, Trey said, "Trev, why didn't you tell me what was going on. Now you've dug a deeper hole for yourself. What charges is he looking at, Tori?" Trey was the only one that shorten Victoria's name. She didn't like it, but gotten used to it.

"Well it seems as though Jackie Brown is accusing Trevor of murdering Tia." Vitoria said.

"What evidence do the police have for picking Trev up?" Trey continued.

"All circumstantial, but adding up quickly. Trey, you're not looking good these days, are you sure you're strong enough to be out and about?" Victoria asked.

"Jerome and Tara will be handling most of the footwork until I regain my strength, but I will not be put on the back burner." Trey said.

"Trey, I appreciate your wiliness to help, but you should be at home, man. I will stop by after I pick up a few things from home." Trevor said.

"Okay, I'm kind of wasted. JW can take me home while you and Tara head over to mom and dads." Trey said, ignoring that Trevor said he would be over later.

"Well, we're done here for now. Enjoy the rest of your weekend Trevor and be at my office first thing Monday morning." Victoria said.

"I'm going to let it drop for now, Tori, but don't think I didn't noticed that you didn't answer my question about what the police have on Trev." Trey said.

"Go home, Trey and get some rest." Victoria instructed.

"See you later, Trev. Tara don't leave mom and dad's until we can get a handle on who else is out there creating problems." Trey left the police station with Jerome to go home to get some much needed rest.

<u>Chapter Seventeen</u>

Tara arrived at the office early Monday morning. The rest of the weekend flew by after the incident at the police station. Trevor was picked up because of the statements both Jackie and Tony Brown made against him. They said that Trevor had murdered Tia because she decided to go back with Tony. They also told the police about Trevor being in possession of Tia's bloody clothes. The duo also said that Trevor was aware of the money, drugs, and clothing that were in Tia's possession.

Trenton and Jerome went with Trevor when he met with Victoria. Trey was upset but knew he had to be sidelined for a while. He wasn't even strong enough to attend church yesterday. What bothered him the most was that he couldn't spend quality time with his son.

Beverly was already at the office when Tara and the two men guarding her arrived. Tara could take care of herself, but she was now fearful of the unknown. Having Jackie and Tony behind bars wasn't enough. Tony was lucky to be alive after the incident involving Trey's shooting. The shooter was killed at the scene, but Tony and another one of his crew only received scratches and bruises from the car wreck.

Tara made sure she was aware of her surroundings and was on alert for anything that may happen. She felt better when Carl told her that Jackie trying to make a plea deal gave him names and other information that may lead to the arrest of several other people involved. He said Jackie bragged about how she and Tony forced Tia to be a part of the smuggling ring. She also admitted to forcing Tia to get identification in Tara's name. They threaten if Tia didn't go along with their plan; they were going to snatch Tara and torture her bit by bit and send her mutilated body to her family.

Tara knew this case was far from over and that danger was still lurking at her doorstep until everyone involved was arrested. Unlike Jackie, Tony wasn't saying anything outside of blaming Trevor for Tia's murder. He blamed Tara for messing up his relationship with Tia and said that she will never be safe from him no matter where he was or what happened to him. Jackie blamed almost everything on Tony and his thug friends. She played innocent. Coming out of her thoughts when the two men guarding her came rushing in, Tara went into defense mold.

"What's going on, guys?" Tara asked.

"There are four or more dudes trying to get in here. The police was already called." One of the guards said.

"Where is Bev?"

"She is locked in the small office in the back."

"Oh God, this can't be happening." Tara said as she called Jerome and told him what was going on. She had no intentions of calling Trey.

"Jerome we're headed into the panic room. There are several men trying to get in." Tara said.

"I know. We are on our way now. I hope you didn't call TT. You know he will try to hop his weak behind down there?" Jerome said.

"Of course I didn't. The last thing I need to hear is Linda's complaining."

"Ok, help is on the way." Jerome said, but he heard the loud noise in the background. "Get out of there right now, Tara."

Tara disconnected the call as she and the two guards went to the back room to get Beverly and headed for the panic room.

By the time Jerome and the police arrived they saw the damaged to the front door and how the assailants must have run away before they arrived. Approaching the area slowly, Jerome, Carl, Keshawn, and two officers observed the scene. Once the all clear was established, Jerome sent the secret code to Tara letting her know it was safe for them to come out.

Tara ran to Jerome and gave him a hug and once she saw Keshawn she went into his arms. Carl asked her if they were okay. He dismissed the officers and told them to go back to the station. Carl explained two of the four people Jackie named were in custody. Of course, the other two on the loose she said were the leaders and the most dangerous. Carl ordered Jerome and Keshawn to take Tara to her parents' house once they were done evaluating the scene. After that Jerome was going to go over to Trey's house to update him on the latest event. Before leaving Carl turned to Tara.

"Now you see why I didn't want you involved in this case, Intern Taylor."

"I know, Captain. I didn't expect it to escalate like this. Now I have to worry about the fallout my brothers have suffered." Tara said.

"Don't worry about Trey, he will pull through this just fine once he regain his strength, Trevor on the other hand my not fair as easily."

"Don't count, Trev out. I know he is in his feelings right now, but he is strong just like the rest of our family."

"I hope you are right. Now go get some rest and stay close to your family. Make sure you don't travel anywhere alone until we have apprehended the other two suspects."

"Will do, Captain." Tara said. They left the office with Carl making sure Beverly made it home safely, while Jerome and Keshawn escorted Tara to her parents.

<u>Chapter Eighteen</u>

It had been a long week. Trey was back in the office after staying away for almost a week. He was much stronger and ready to put this case to bed. He was amazingly calm when Jerome told him about the upheaval that happened at the firm on Monday. Trevor had been working with Trey all week to help him regain his strength. This was good for Trevor too because now he seemed to be more calm even though he wasn't out of the woods in Tia's murder case.

Victoria told Trevor not too worry too much because if they had enough evidence to arrest him they would have done so, but she made Trevor promise not to keep anything else from her or she would drop his case. Trey thought Victoria was being hard on Trevor, but Trey knew he couldn't say too much because they needed her. Now sitting at the office, Trey wondered if this case was almost over since they had apprehended all the suspects Jackie named. His thoughts were interrupted when Linda knocked on his door. She came in and set in one of the chairs across from Trey's desk.

"What brings you here, baby?" Trey asked.

"You're not going to believe what happened to me earlier today." Linda said.

Trey was on alert. Linda didn't look upset, but he wondered if someone had tried to mess with her. "I'm listening, baby."

"Well, I had just put the baby down for his nap when the doorbell rang." Linda stopped. This made Trey anxious.

"Don't leave me in suspense." Trey said calmly.

"Okay, let me talk. I answered the door because Mrs. Moore was out running errands and Tara was on the other side."

"Tara, I thought she was at the police station training."

"She was headed there and decided to stop in to see me first. Of course my guard was up. I didn't feel like fighting with her but to my surprise she came in and gave me a big hug. I was speechless." Linda said.

Trey was too for the moment. "What was that about?"

"Well, she said she had made amends with Talia and it was my turn. She said after all that has happened and you getting hurt, it was time she grew up." Linda explained.

"How did you receive this information?"

"Once I was able to form words, I looked at her closely to see if she was serious."

"And after that, what happened?"

"Well, I told her it was about time we both started to grow up. We both know how important you are to us and when it boils down to it neither of us wanted to put you in the position to choose between the two of us."

"Wow, I wished I was a fly on the wall to see your faces."

"We know that it still going to take time. She said she was very proud of you because you loved her enough to give Keshawn a chance when she first started dating him."

"I may have been wrong about him. To be honest I didn't want to lose Tara so that was one of the reasons why I gave him a hard time." Trey said.

"Well, she had to get to work so she wanted the four of us to get together soon. She said that she will do her best to loosen her grip on you. She also said she is ready to focus on having a closer relationship with Keshawn."

"Well, I still don't think those two are ready for marriage right now. She hinted at this before all of this happened with Tia. I guess I was in my feelings at the time because I was kind of short with her."

"I think Tara isn't the only one that needs to loosen the grip. I know how important she is to you, Trey, but you have to give her the freedom to make her own choices, Trey."

With a smile on his face Trey said, "I think someone needs to take their own advice. It wasn't too long ago that a similar situation happened to you."

"Well, I was right about that girl. She didn't love my brother. She just saw him as a meal ticket. I'm just glad she dumped him before the "I do's." Linda said.

"Okay, time for me to get back to work. See you at home later, baby." Trey walked Linda to her car before getting back to work.

Tara, Trey, and Jerome was working in the conference room when Beverly peeked her head into the door and told them that Carl and Keshawn was there to see them. Tara was surprised because when she talked to Carl earlier he didn't have any new details in Tia's case. Instead of wondering what they were there about, the trio waited patiently for their visitors to be escorted in. Tara smiled every time

Keshawn walked into the room. She knew Trey might not like it, but she was ready to settle down with Keshawn. She wasn't going to live with him without being married, so she decided it was time for them to talk seriously about getting married. Her thoughts were interrupted.

"Intern Taylor, gentlemen, I thought you guys would like to hear this update in person." Carl said.

"I appreciate that, Captain." Tara said.

"Well, we can finally add Ms. Thomas' case to the closed file."

"Oh my God, so that means I can return home?" Tara asked.

"If that is your wish, Intern Taylor" Carl responded.

"So what happened, Captain?"

"The killer turned herself in this morning.

"Oh my, God, this is great." Tara paused, "You said her?" Tara asked.

"Yes, one of Mr. Brown's female friends" Carl explained.

"That's great news, now Trev is off the hook." Trey said.

"Yes he is. We never suspected him of anything, but falling for a troubled young woman." Carl said.

"Please continue, Captain?" Tara said.

"On the night that Tia left your brother's gym, Mr. Brown arranged for her to meet with him. Tia was unaware she was meeting with Mr. Brown. She thought she was meeting with the head guy she was running drugs for and boosting clothes." Carl paused. "Never meeting him before and only hearing his voice through a voice changer, Ms. Thomas didn't realize Mr. Brown was the big boss."

"You mean to tell me that idiot was able to pull that off?" Tara asked.

"Yes, he was. He would have gotten away with it too if the killer didn't turn herself in this morning." Keshawn said.

"How did she know to try to set up Trev for the murder?" Jerome asked.

"Mr. Brown found out on the day of the meeting that Tia had been in a relationship with Mr. Taylor, and went ballistic. He knew that was the reason why he wasn't able to talk her into coming back to him like he had many times before. He also was mad because he wasn't able to find out where she hid the money and merchandise." Carl explained.

"The killer said when Tia was brought to the location she was hiding and heard Mr. Brown begging Tia to come back to him. When she refused he beat and raped her. While she was unconscious Mr. Brown left her in what he thought was an empty building with plans on returning for her later." Carl nodded to Keshawn to take over.

"When Tia came to and was about to leave the killer confronted her. She overpowered Tia. After a few minutes of the ladies fighting, Tia found a wooden plank and hit her attacker."

"Damn, she couldn't catch a break." Tara said under her breath.

"Anyway, that is when the killer pulled a gun on Tia and shot her four times in the chest." Keshawn continued. "The killer said she was scared of what Tony was going to do to her so she removed most of Tia's clothes and dumped her body in the park. When Tony found out what she did, he helped her to set up Trevor using the bloody clothes and sent her into hiding."

"So it was Tony that made Tia get the fake ID and do all the illegal activities?" Tara asked.

"Yes. He blamed Ms. Thomas breaking up with him on you. He was also mad about your brother's involvement with Ms. Thomas. We have to head back to the station now. I'm sorry for your loss again, Intern Taylor." Carl said.

"Captain, are you ever going to call me, Tara." Tara asked.

"Probably not, or maybe when you move up through the ranks." Carl responded.

"I'm going to hold you to that, Captain." Tara said her goodbyes and went to the restroom to have a good cry.

Epilogue

Four months later

Tara was nervous. She thought this day would never get here. Sitting in the room surrounded by the most important women in her life, Tara thought back to the time a few months back when she asked Trey not her dad for permission to marry Keshawn. She made Trey promised not to tell anyone even Linda that she asked him first. She wanted her dad's approval, but she felt she needed Trey's more.

After Trey gave his approval she told the rest of her family about her engagement. She had gotten closer to Linda and asked her to be one of the bridesmaids. This made Trey happy. The best surprise for the family was that she asked Talia to be her matron of honor. Although Tara had other friends, none of them were close enough to her for that honor. She wished Tia was there other than in spirit.

Tara being Tara had some non-traditional moments added to her wedding, the biggest being that Trey was going to walk her half-way down the church isle then her dad would take over the rest of the way. She also had the reception before the wedding. The main reason was that Keshawn's parents couldn't make the wedding so they had the reception a week early.

When Time Runs Out: Tara's Quest for Vengeance

Tara was happy for Trevor whose formal girl-friend from high school moved back into town and now they were happy as two peas in a pod. She had a feeling that another Taylor wedding was going to be around the corner. Talia's two daughters were the flower girls while her son was the ring bearer. As soon as the wedding was over, Tara and Keshawn were going on their honeymoon to Jamaica. This was a wedding gift from Trey and Linda.

Thinking back to the close of the case, Tara was mostly happy about the outcome. She didn't like the fact that Jackie Brown was sentence to only five years. The good news was, Tony, his goons, and the lady that murdered Tia all received life without parole. Tara felt Tia could finally rest in peace. Her best friend would always be close in Tara's heart, but she knew it was time for her to move on to a new chapter in her life.

Leaving her dressing room and meeting Trey at the back of the church was a dream come true for Tara. When it was time for Trey to hand Tara over to their dad, Tara gave Trey a thumbs up sign. Looking towards the altar, where Talia and Keshawn's best friend was waiting, Tara was almost speechless. Her final glance around the church, Tara thought to herself, *Vengeance is best served sunny side up."*

Questions

Listed below are some potential questions that can be used for a book club discussion:

<u>Story/Characters</u>

1. What was the most important scene in the book? Would it have made the book less important if the scene wasn't in there?

2. Were there any storylines in the book that was surprising or stood out? If yes what were they?

3. Did you find any of the storylines predicable? If yes which ones?

4. Was there any point in the book where you disagreed with the main character actions?

5. Did you see any changes or transformations in the main character?

6. Was it hard to relate to any of the characters in this book?

7. Do you think it was wrong that Tara was involved in Tia's murder case?

8. What are your thoughts about Tara and Talia's relationship?

9. Do you know of any siblings that are as close as Tara and Trey?

10. Was it surprising about Trevor's involvement with Tia?

11. What was the best scene in the book?

12. Do you think Tara's character showed growth and improvements by the end?

<u>Overall</u>

1. Have you read any other books by Diana Carter? If yes, how were they compared to this book?

2. What if anything did you learn or take away from this book?

3. Did you have any preconceptions about this book before you read it?

4. As you read the book, did your opinion change? If so, how?

5. What would you like to see this author do next?

6. How would you rate the author's overall storytelling abilities?

9 780999 710661